What If It Never Stops Raining?

By Nancy Carlson

Viking

Dedicated to
the memory of my friend
Michael Blake

VIKING
Published by the Penguin Group
Penguin Books USA Inc.,
375 Hudson Street, New York 10014, U.S.A.
Penguin Books Ltd, 27 Wrights Lane, London W8 5TZ, England
Penguin Books Australia Ltd, Ringwood, Victoria, Australia
Penguin Books Canada Ltd, 10 Alcorn Avenue, Toronto, Ontario, Canada M4V 3B2
Penguin Books (N.Z.) Ltd, 182–190 Wairau Road, Auckland 10, New Zealand

Penguin Books Ltd, Registered Offices: Harmondsworth, Middlesex, England

First published in 1992 by Viking Penguin, a division of Penguin Books USA Inc.

1 3 5 7 9 10 8 6 4 2

Library of Congress Cataloging-in-Publication Data
Carlson, Nancy L.
What if it never stops raining? / by Nancy Carlson.   p.   cm.
Summary: Tim is always worrying about something, but things never
turn out as badly as he thinks they will.
ISBN 0-670-81775-9
[1. Worry—Fiction.]   I. Title.   PZ7.C21665Wh   1992   [E]—dc20   91-48176   CIP   AC
Printed in Hong Kong
Set in Veljovic

Tim is a worrier. When it rains
he worries about floods.

"What if it never stops raining?
Our house will be swept away.
We will have to cling to our roof.
It will be horrible," said Tim.

"Honey, we've never had a flood," said Mom.
"But if we do, we could jump in a boat
    and sail down the street.

"We could keep sailing until we found a tropical island. You could fish and play in the sand."

"Boy, that sounds great,"
said Tim.
But then, after an hour, guess what?

It stopped raining.

"Darn! I wanted to sail to an island," said Tim.

When it was time for school, Tim worried
when he saw a new bus driver behind the wheel.

"What if the new driver gets lost and

we never see our homes and parents again?'' said Tim.

"But if we do get lost, we'll get
to miss science class!" said Katie.

They made it to school
just in time for science.

In science class Tim worried
about giving his oral report
on the parts of a flower.

"What if I forget my report?
 What if I'm too nervous to speak?"
 worried Tim.

"Then the whole class will
laugh at you!" said Patrick.

But Tim did fine. He was glad he practiced so much
the night before. He remembered all the flower parts,
and Mr. Stotts said he did a great job.

At recess Tim and Patrick climbed to the top of the swing set.

"Let's hang by our knees," said Patrick.

Katie said, "That sounds dangerous!"

Tim thought Katie was right. He worried he might
fall and get hurt. So he decided to climb down.
"Chicken," said Patrick.

Patrick hung by his knees, fell off,
and got a huge bump on his head.

After school Tim had a baseball game.
"What if I strike out? Then the whole
team will get mad at me and

22

I'll get kicked off the team,'' worried Tim.
"But you might hit a home run
and win the game,'' said Dad.

"A major league scout will sign you!"

"Dad, Dad! Get real," said Tim.

Well, Tim did strike out.

But no one got mad at him.

After the game everyone went out for pizza.
"You'll do better next time," said the coach.

As Tim got ready for bed
he thought about the day.

"I had a pretty good day after all,"
he told his mom. "It did stop raining,
my report went great, we had a fun ball-game,
and I didn't do anything dumb like Patrick."

"You see, you don't have to worry
about everything," said Mom.
"But what if—" Tim began.

"Stop. No more worries, Tim!
There are no monsters waiting under
your bed. Just go to sleep," said Mom.

"Gee, all I wanted to know was
what if I get thirsty during the night?
I hadn't thought about monsters . . ."
But Tim was too tired to worry.

Instead, Tim fell fast asleep.